Baseball Legends

Hank Aaron
Grover Cleveland Alexander
Ernie Banks
Albert Belle
Johnny Bench
Yogi Berra
Barry Bonds
Roy Campanella
Roberto Clemente
Ty Cobb
Dizzy Dean
Joe DiMaggio
Bob Feller
Jimmie Foxx
Lou Gehrig
Bob Gibson
Ken Griffey, Jr.
Rogers Hornsby
Walter Johnson
Sandy Koufax
Greg Maddux
Mickey Mantle
Christy Mathewson
Willie Mays
Stan Musial
Satchel Paige
Mike Piazza
Cal Ripken, Jr.
Brooks Robinson
Frank Robinson
Jackie Robinson
Babe Ruth
Tom Seaver
Duke Snider
Warren Spahn
Willie Stargell
Frank Thomas
Honus Wagner
Ted Williams
Carl Yastrzemski
Cy Young

Chelsea House Publishers

BASEBALL LEGENDS

BARRY BONDS

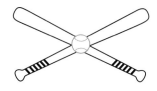

Carrie Muskat

Introduction by
Jim Murray

Senior Consultant
Earl Weaver

CHELSEA HOUSE PUBLISHERS
Philadelphia

Cover photo credit: AP/Wide World Photo

Produced by Choptank Syndicate, Inc.

Editor and Picture Researcher: Norman L. Macht
Production Coordinator and Editorial Assistant: Mary E. Hull
Designer: Lisa Hochstein
Cover Designer: Alison Burnside

1 3 5 7 9 8 6 4 2

Library of Congress Cataloging-in-Publication Data

Muskat, Carrie.
      Barry Bonds / Carrie Muskat: introduction by Jim Murray;
senior consultant, Earl Weaver.
         p. cm. — (Baseball legends)
        Includes bibliographical references and index.
        Summary: A biography of the San Francisco Giants outfielder
who came to prominence in the 1990s.
        ISBN 0-7910-4376-2
        1. Bonds, Barry, 1964- —Juvenile literature.
2. Baseball players—United States—Biography—Juvenile
literature. [1. Bonds, Barry, 1964- . 2. Baseball
players. 3. Afro-Americans—Biography.] I. Title.
II. Series.
GV865.B63M87 1997
796.357'092—dc21
    [B]   97-1678
                                                CIP
                                                    AC

CONTENTS

WHAT MAKES A STAR

Jim Murray

No one has ever been able to explain to me the mysterious alchemy that makes one man a .350 hitter and another player, more or less identical in physical makeup, hard put to hit .200. You look at an Al Kaline, who played with the Detroit Tigers from 1953 to 1974. He was pale, stringy, almost poetic-looking. He always seemed to be struggling against a bad case of mononucleosis. But with a bat in his hands, he was King Kong. During his career, he hit 399 home runs, rapped out 3,007 hits, and compiled a .297 batting average.

Form isn't the reason. The first time anybody saw Roberto Clemente step into the batter's box for the Pittsburgh Pirates, the best guess was that Clemente would be back in Double A ball in a week. He had one foot in the bucket and held his bat at an awkward angle—he looked as though he couldn't hit an outside pitch. A lot of other ballplayers may have had a better-looking stance. Yet they never led the National League in hitting in four different years, the way Clemente did.

Not every ballplayer is born with the ability to hit a curveball. Nor is exceptional hand-eye coordination the key to heavy hitting. Big league locker rooms are filled with players who have all the attributes, save one: discipline. Every baseball man can tell you a story about a pitcher who throws a ball faster than anyone has ever seen but who has no control on or *off* the field.

The Hall of Fame is full of people who transformed themselves into great ballplayers by working at the sport, by studying the game, and making sacrifices. They're overachievers—and winners. If you want to find them, just watch the World Series. Or simply read about New York Yankee great Lou Gehrig; Ted Williams, "the Splendid Splinter" of the Boston Red Sox; or the Dodgers' strikeout king Sandy Koufax.

A pitcher *should* be able to win a lot of ballgames with a 98-miles-per-hour fastball. But what about the pitcher who wins 20 games a year with a fastball so slow that you can catch it with your teeth? Bob Feller of the Cleveland Indians got into the Hall of Fame with a blazing fastball that glowed in the dark. National League star Grover Cleveland Alexander got there with a pitch that took considerably longer to reach the plate; but when it did arrive, the pitch was exactly where Alexander wanted it to be—and the last place the batter expected it to be.

There are probably more players with exceptional ability who didn't make it to the major leagues than there are who did. A number of great hitters, bored with fielding practice, had to be dropped from their team because their home-run production didn't make up for their lapses in the field. And then there are players like Brooks Robinson of the Baltimore Orioles, who made himself into a human vacuum cleaner at third base because he knew that working hard to become an expert fielder would win him a job in the big leagues.

A star is not something that flashes through the sky. That's a comet. Or a meteor. A star is something you can steer ships by. It stays in place and gives off a steady glow; it is fixed, permanent. A star works at being a star.

And that's how you tell a star in baseball. He shows up night after night and takes pride in how brightly he shines. He's Willie Mays running so hard his hat keeps falling off; Ty Cobb sliding to stretch a single into a double; Lou Gehrig, after being fooled in his first two at-bats, belting the next pitch off the light tower because he's taken the time to study the pitcher. Stars never take themselves for granted. That's why they're stars.

1

THE 30–30 CLUB

"I am going to be the person I am."
— Barry Bonds

Barry Bonds had heard it enough: like father, like son. His father, Bobby Bonds, had played 14 seasons in the major leagues and was the only five-time 30–30 player (30 homers and 30 stolen bases in a single season). Barry was expected to do the same as soon as he got to the big leagues in 1986 with the Pittsburgh Pirates: hit like his dad, run like his dad, be a superstar like his dad. "Barry faced a different kind of pressure," said Bobby Bonilla, Barry's teammate in Pittsburgh. "He had to live up to the legend of Bobby Bonds."

Fans would yell "Bobby! Bobby!" whenever Barry walked by, confusing his name with his father's. It bothered the young Bonds because he wanted to establish his own identity.

"Why do I have to live up to anybody's expectations?" he would say.

Celebrity parents often find themselves in an uncomfortable position, knowing that they are setting a high standard that others may expect their children to match. In the early 1970s, Bobby Bonds was considered by some to be one of the most complete players in baseball and everyone expected his son to be just as talented. Barry

Barry Bonds breaks from home as all eyes follow the flight of the ball. In 1990 that scene was played out often as Bonds hit 33 home runs and batted .301. He also stole 53 bases to become the second player ever to reach 30 homers and 50 steals in a season.

Bonds was quickly labeled as having the potential to be as good or better than his dad. Yet potential can be a millstone around one's neck.

In Barry's first three seasons in Pittsburgh, he failed to live up to his family name. He had averaged 23 home runs and 27 stolen bases 1987–89, and had been the only player in the National League to score more than 95 runs in each of those years. Yet he had a .103 batting average with runners in scoring position late in games, the lowest ever charted by the baseball statisticians at Elias Sports Bureau. "Barry's at the point where he should be," said Pirates manager Jim Leyland, trying to deflect some of the criticism.

Bonds was the Pirates' leadoff batter, but he resented that role. His father had batted first; that did not mean he had to do the same. It made him look like he was falling short of the standards placed on someone with such baseball bloodlines.

Sportswriters had always talked about Bonds' potential when he did not play the way they thought he should. "People wanted superstardom from me right from Jump Street and wouldn't let up on me for just being good," Bonds said. "They never really got it that my dad was bigger and stronger and didn't have to work at it. He just walked up to the plate and boom."

Despite batting a disappointing .248 in 1989—to a great extent the result of a failed attempt during the last month and a half to hit his 20th home run—Bonds had asked for a salary of $1.6 million for 1990. The Pirates offered $850,000, and an arbitrator decided the team's offer was fair. The Pittsburgh media labeled Bonds as "the Pirates' MDP—Most Despised Player." Barry became resentful of everyone's expectations. He spent the off-season in the weight room, getting stronger, both physically and mentally. He wanted to be more than just Bobby Bonds' son. "I decided this year it was time for me to get the respect I deserved for myself," he said.

"Most guys who talk about what they're going to do, they usually set themselves up to get humbled," Leyland said. "Barry Bonds was like Joe Namath and Muhammad Ali. He could make a statement and go out and back it up. Not a lot of guys can do that. In fact, managers usually cringe when guys make statements about what they're going to do. In Barry's case, I liked it. I think he did it on purpose to motivate himself. In a lot of ways, it's easy for Barry. I think he needs a little controversy around him."

Leyland decided to change the Pirates lineup for the 1990 season. Instead of Bonds batting leadoff, he was dropped to the No. 5 spot. Jeff King, Jay Bell, Andy Van Slyke and Bonilla would hit ahead of Bonds. With runners on base, Bonds flourished. By the All-Star break, he had driven in 62 runs to top his previous full-season high of 58 RBI. He was able to combine the unique skills of a leadoff batter—getting on base, aggressively stealing—with that of a run-producer.

"I don't think Barry became the player he is without Leyland," Bonilla said. "He [Leyland] had this incredible knack for making sure you were very successful. He always made sure your confidence was up."

When the first-place Pirates arrived in Chicago for a three-game series in mid-September, the New York Mets were on their heels in the National League East. Bonds had 29 home runs and 48 stolen bases at that point. All he needed was one more homer to join the elite 30–30 club.

Switch-hitter Bobby Bonilla and Bonds— the "Killer B's"—led the Pittsburgh Pirates to three straight National League East titles, but they never made it to the World Series. By 1993 Bonds and Bonilla had gone separate ways as free agents when the small-market Pirates could not afford to keep them.

On September 18, the Pirates faced the Cubs' ace Greg Maddux. Every at-bat on that crisp autumn night, Bonds tried to launch a pitch out over the ivy-covered outfield walls. But Maddux shut him down four times and the Cubs won 8–5. The next day, Bonds took a different approach. He relaxed, didn't think about 30–30, forgot the expectations and the comparisons to his father. Baseball's a game, he realized. It was supposed to be fun.

In the first inning, Bonds flew out to right. He drew a walk in the third. But with two out in the fifth and the Pirates ahead 4–1, Bonds launched a towering drive to right off Cubs reliever Bill Long. With that majestic swing, Pittsburgh had its first 30–30 player.

"I just wanted to run off the field, call my dad and say, 'It's over with,'" said Bonds, who added his 31st home run leading off the seventh for good measure. The Pirates won 8–7, and the next day, Bonds connected on his 32nd home run in an 11–2 victory over the Cubs.

"I want to put my father and myself in an untouchable class as a father-son combination," Bonds said. "When my dad was doing it [30–30], it was only him and Willie Mays. Besides, he told me it was no big deal then. It was expected, and you didn't get paid extra for it."

He was the best player in baseball that year, and the Pirates—fueled by the "Killer B's," Bonds and Bonilla—won the National League East. Bonds finished with a .301 average, hit 33 home runs and drove in 114 runs. He stole 53 bases to become only the second player in baseball to go 30–50. Cincinnati's Eric Davis also hit 30 homers and stole 50 bases in 1987. "I can't imagine anyone playing better than Barry played," Leyland said. "It was like he went out to prove how good he was."

Bonds finally did something his father never did. He became the first major leaguer ever to have at least 30 homers, 100 RBI, 100 runs scored and 50 stolen bases in a single season. And, he won the Most Valuable Player award by a near unanimous vote. Barry Bonds dedicated the season to his dad. "You know what I'm proudest of?" Bobby Bonds said. "That now I'm known as Barry Bonds's father."

But the brash young Bonds wasn't going to win any popularity contests. "Barry can be very arrogant," said teammate R. J. Reynolds. "He can really tick you off. But then, maybe that's his strength. One day, he's the greatest person in the world; the next, he won't talk to you."

Bonds wanted to be the best, and he didn't care what anyone thought about him.

"I am going to be the person I am," Barry Bonds said.

And he meant it.

2

THE NEXT
WILLIE MAYS

"Dad, they think I'm cocky."
— Barry Bonds

The number 24 was significant to Barry Bonds. He was born on July 24, 1964, in Riverside, California, to his mother, Patricia, and father, Bobby. Just 11 days after he was born, his father signed his first big league contract with the San Francisco Giants. Because of his strength and speed, people started comparing Bobby Bonds with another Giants outfielder, Willie Mays, who wore No. 24.

Bobby Bonds did not get called up to the big leagues until 1968, but he made quite an impression. He hit a grand slam in his first game, June 25, 1968, against Los Angeles. Bobby Bonds hit 30 home runs and stole 30 bases in five seasons, the only ballplayer to do so.

"I knew I could do anything on a baseball field that any other man could do," Bobby said. "As a leadoff hitter, I drove in 100 runs. As a leadoff hitter, I hit 30 homers. As a leadoff hitter, I stole 30 bases. I never hit 40 homers—39 was the most— but I was supposed to do that because Willie Mays did. Expectations people have for you can't dictate your future for you." Bobby Bonds passed that message on to his oldest son Barry later in

Barry Bonds' father, Bobby, was a tough act to follow. In his 14-year career, Bobby Bonds reached 30 home runs and 30 stolen bases five times. Here he has just been tagged out in a steal attempt for the California Angels in 1976.

life. Young Barry grew up at the ballpark amid high expectations. Because the Bonds family lived just 20 minutes from Candlestick Park where the Giants played, Patricia would drive 4-year-old Barry, his 3-year-old brother Ricky and their dad to the stadium before home games. The youngsters were free to roam the clubhouse and would join the big leaguers like Willie McCovey and Willie Mays in the outfield during batting practice, chasing down balls and trying to catch as many as they could.

"I took Barry everywhere," Bobby Bonds said.

The giant-sized playground was home for Barry and Ricky. They were not intimidated by the size of the field or the big men moving around them or the sharp noise of the bat hitting the hard ball. Barry became hooked. "He definitely took to baseball at an early age," said his mother Patricia. "He could hit the ball from the first day he lifted the bat. You'd walk in the door and he'd get a bat and ball and make you pitch to him."

Barry learned more than just playing the game. "The cutest thing I remember about Barry in those days was him signing autographs," his mother said. "Barry and Ricky would wait behind the fence outside the clubhouse with all the other youngsters. When kids couldn't get Bobby's autograph, they'd settle for Barry's or Ricky's."

Signing autographs was easy. But being a good ballplayer required more than good genes. At least seven Hall of Famers had had sons who tried to be ballplayers. None became stars. One veteran minor league manager, Harry Bright, recalled, "I saw [Rogers] Hornsby's kid. He couldn't play a lick. Hank Greenberg's kid was terrible. Mickey Mantle's kids played a year or so in Class D ball and that was it."

However, young Barry's ability became evident very early. When he was 7 years old, he hit a home run to win a farm league game. "It rolled right through everybody and I got around the bases," he recalled. "That was the start of my career right there."

At Candlestick Park, Barry followed Willie Mays everywhere, and not just because Mays was Barry's godfather. "My father was just my father," he would say later. "He was my favorite because he was my father, but I loved to watch Willie Mays."

Hall of Famer Willie Mays, a teammate of Bobby Bonds's on the San Francisco Giants, was young Barry's hero. Mays, who hit 660 home runs, was a sensational center fielder and baserunner who played the game with exuberance. Barry chose Mays's number 24 to wear.

Bobby Bonds saw the way his son worshiped Mays. It did not bother him. "I was just Dad going to work," he said. "I was a guy with a job. Mays was his hero."

Barry had chosen well. Mays, the Giants' "Say Hey Kid," played the game with enthusiasm and exuberance. Fans cheered when his cap would fly off as he sprinted after fly balls that few other outfielders could reach. He excelled at everything: hitting for average and power, fielding, and baserunning. His staggering career statistics include 3,283 hits, 660 home runs and a .302 average. A two-time Most Valuable Player, Mays won 11 Gold Gloves and appeared in 24 All-Star Games before his playing days ended in 1973.

This was the legend that Bobby Bonds was supposed to match when he joined the Giants in 1968. During his seven seasons in San Francisco, Bonds was good enough for veteran Cincinnati manager Sparky Anderson to call him the best player in the country. But to many Giants fans, Bonds was a failure because he did not come up to Mays's level of stardom.

Bobby Bonds left that behind him when he went to the New York Yankees in 1975. He continued to hit for power and steal bases while playing for seven teams in the next seven years.

When Barry was in Little League, wearing the same number 24 as Mays, he was far ahead of his teammates because of the time he had spent in big league ballparks mingling with and watching the best players. In addition to observing how the game should be played, he had learned one other valuable lesson that stayed with him: "Everybody has their own way. You can learn things from watching other people, but you can never be them. When my dad came up to the Giants, everybody said he was going to be the next Willie Mays, but in the end they just called him Bobby Bonds."

Barry's superior athletic skills helped him star at basketball and football at Serra High School in San Mateo, California. Serra High had a strong athletic tradition. Former NFL wide receiver Lynn Swann, major league baseball player and manager Jim Fregosi and pro ballplayer Gregg Jefferies also went to the same high school. "I loved to play football but I hated to get hit," Barry said. "I just didn't have that mad desire. I didn't want to get hurt and I didn't want to hurt anyone. When I used to get hit, man, I'd want to strangle that dude. I'd want to get the ball back and go back there and hit him so hard, but I lost that. In basketball, I loved that, too, but only if I could shoot from way outside or slam dunk. I was constantly thinking about being quick on my feet.

"Baseball has given me an outlet for both those feelings," Bonds said. "I can play angry, like when I throw home from center field. I can put a lot of anger in that throw. I can be quick on my feet, like when we need to steal a base."

"You could see the talent was there the minute he stepped on the field as a freshman," said Dave Stevens, then the Serra High baseball coach. "I saw him hit the ball out of the park as a freshman. He was on the varsity three years and we were the champions his sophomore and junior seasons. Barry was so eager to learn— he'd have played all day if I let him." During the playoffs his junior year, Barry had 10 hits in 16 at bats, including three home runs and 12 RBI. Baseball came easy to Barry, but he also recognized that his talent alienated him from his friends. "I could call my shots," he said. "I could tell you when I was going to hit a homer. It got to the point where I could do pretty much what I wanted and then I'd shut it down because it was causing problems. I wanted to do well but I didn't want to show up my buddies."

Bonds hit .404 over three varsity seasons, and hit an incredible .467 in his senior year when he was named to a prep All-America team. Four or five major league scouts attended every one of Barry's games that year. Before one game, a scout for the St. Louis Cardinals asked coach Stevens if he would let Barry use a wooden bat for one at-bat. High schoolers were using aluminum bats at that time but major league players use wood. "Barry went along with it and he hit a ball clear over the right field wall and into the sand dunes, which was quite a poke," Stevens said. Barry definitely had major league power.

Bobby Bonds missed most of Barry's high school games because of his commitment to baseball and because he did not want to encourage comparisons between the two. The elder Bonds ended his playing career in 1982. He played for the Giants, Yankees, California Angels, Chicago White Sox, Texas Rangers, Cleveland Indians, St. Louis Cardinals and Chicago Cubs over 14 seasons, hitting 332 home runs and stealing 461 bases.

When Barry Bonds graduated from high school, he had learned from the best; because of that, he felt he was better than most. It was an attitude young Barry had noticed in star players.

"He'll say, 'Dad, they think I'm cocky,'" Bobby Bonds said. "I tell him you can't go around flaunting it, but you have to be confident. Just demonstrate it. If people can't handle that, then they have a problem. I've never seen a good ballplayer, a Roberto Clemente, a Willie Mays, who didn't know he was a good ballplayer."

Barry Bonds knew he was good. Now he had to show everyone else.

3

MAKING THE BIG LEAGUES

"He gave you goose bumps."
— scout Angel Figueroa

When he was only 17, Barry Bonds was chosen in the second round of the June 1982 draft by the San Francisco Giants. It was the same team his father had played for from 1968 to 1974. The Giants offered him a $75,000 bonus but Bobby Bonds thought that was $5,000 short—the cost of a college education at that time—and Barry wanted to go to school. Instead of joining the Giants' rookie league team, Barry accepted a full scholarship at Arizona State University.

Arizona State had a strong baseball tradition. Perennial contenders at the College World Series, ASU players often were first-round draft picks, beginning with Rick Monday, who was selected in the inaugural free-agent draft in 1965.

Bonds was not a normal freshman ballplayer. He had grown up in major league ballparks and learned from the best in the game. Confident beyond his young age, he eagerly offered hitting tips to other players.

"Barry did things that were amazing," said major league outfielder Mike Devereaux, who played with Bonds in Arizona State's outfield for two years. "He would hit a ball with topspin over

At Arizona State University, Bonds played in the same outfield with future major leaguers Mike Devereaux and Oddibe McDowell. Growing up among big league players gave Bonds an edge over his teammates. It also gave him a bragging, arrogant attitude that made him no friends.

the fence that would be incredible. A ball like that would usually drop in front of the outfielder, but instead his went over the fences."

But Bonds' brashness bothered some of his teammates. "I never saw a teammate care about him," said Arizona State coach Jim Brock. "Part of it would be his being rude, inconsiderate and self-centered. He bragged about the money he turned down and popped off about his dad. I don't think he ever figured out what to do to get people to like him." Brock did not play favorites. During a team trip to Hawaii, Brock told his players not to surf because he wanted them to avoid injuries. Bonds ignored the rules, grabbed a board and splashed in the Pacific Ocean. He paid the price and was suspended from the team. The other players voted not to have him return.

"Arrogant? Yes, he was arrogant," Devereaux said. "But saying he's arrogant is not putting Barry Bonds down."

Angel Figueroa had heard all of the stories. "That didn't concern me," said Figueroa, a long-time scout with the Pittsburgh Pirates. "I was more interested in him as a ballplayer." He started taking notes on Bonds during his freshman year at ASU. College rules prohibited any team from drafting or signing players until after their junior year, but Figueroa did not hesitate. He knew Bonds possessed a unique talent; sure, he was cocky, but he was also a gifted athlete.

Figueroa knew Barry Bonds was in a different category. He was impressed by Bonds' demeanor, the way he swung the bat, the way he hit left-handers better than right-handers. "He's going to be as good as he wants to be," Figueroa said.

At nearly all of the Sun Devils games, Figueroa was in the stands to keep an eye on the left fielder. ASU had a talented outfield in Bonds, Devereaux and Oddibe McDowell, who was the team MVP in Bonds' sophomore year. Yet Bonds outclassed everyone. "He was very aggressive and took advantage of his running speed," Figueroa noted. "He got on base and stole at will. He was a guy who you were always waiting for him to jump out and bite you and do exciting things and give you goose bumps."

Figueroa kept filing reports back to Pittsburgh on Bobby Bonds' son, and convinced one of the Pirates officials to attend a game. But there were no goose bumps on this day. Bonds struck out in three consecutive at-bats on nine pitches.

"What do you think?" Figueroa's boss said.

"He'll be better than you think he is," Figueroa said.

That one game may have been the only time Bonds disappointed the Sun Devils. He batted .347, hit 45 home runs and drove in 175 runs over three seasons. In his sophomore season, he tied an NCAA record with seven consecutive hits in the College World Series.

Even as a teenager, Bonds thrived on pressure situations. "He's the type of guy who will rise to the occasion," Figueroa said. "You get a bunch of guys around who are good or better and he wants to prove he's as good or better. There are guys with more power, there's guys who can run better, guys who can throw better, guys who can hit better. But there's only one guy who can carry the mantle for all of them and that's Barry in my book."

Bonds looked incredibly fast on the bases, but Figueroa needed a 40-yard dash time to show his bosses that he wasn't exaggerating. Bonds was in Chicago and Figueroa asked another scout

Bonds played less than one full season in the minor leagues before the Pirates brought him up in May 1986. He was good and he knew it, and that caused him some problems. "He's his own biggest enemy," Pirates pitcher Rick Reuschel said.

to time the speed test. Barry arrived, driving a convertible and wearing tennis shoes. He did not even warm up, just hopped out of the car and ran the 40 in 6.4 seconds.

The scout was so stunned at the amazing speed, he asked Bonds to run again.

"No," Bonds said. "That's enough."

And he drove away.

But the Pirates did not let him get away. They selected Bonds, just one month shy of his 21st birthday, in the first round of the June 1985 draft, the sixth player taken overall. Many thought Barry could have been the No. 1 pick in the country that year if he did not have a reputation for being a little too cocky.

The comparisons to Bonds' famous father started immediately. Could Barry match or exceed Bobby Bonds' blend of speed and power? "It's a little too early to tell if he will do that," said Pirates general manager Joe L. Brown. "He might steal 30 bases every year and he'll hit his share of home runs, but we don't project him as a home run hitter." Little did they know.

Bonds was speechless when he was drafted, but that was because of Novacain. He had had his wisdom teeth removed that day and could barely talk. But he was speaking just fine when Figueroa went to the Bonds' home in San Mateo, California, to sign the youngster to his first big league contract. The contract talks were anything but smooth. The Pirates made their first offer.

"It's not enough," Barry said.

"Fine," Figueroa said. "Tell me how much money you need."

Bonds wrote a figure on a piece of paper and gave it to Figueroa, who presented it to his bosses.

"Give it to him," they said.

Figueroa knew Bonds was a risk because of his attitude, but the problems seemed to occur off the field, not between the white lines. The Pirates were interested in Bonds the ballplayer.

Assigned to Prince William in the Class A Carolina League, Bonds did not disappoint, batting .299 with 13 homers and 15 stolen bases. He spent the off-season playing winter ball in Venezuela and was promoted the next season to the Class AAA Hawaii Islanders in the Pacific Coast League. Playing for the Islanders was different from playing for any other minor league team. The players lived in a resort-like setting, staying at a small hotel near a beach. They had fresh pineapple and mangoes to eat in the clubhouse, not just cold cuts like other teams. The closest team to the Islanders was in Phoenix, Arizona; every two weeks, the team would fly 2,500 miles to the mainland to play a series of games against other Pacific Coast League teams.

"He always wanted to fit in," said Ed Farmer, a broadcaster for the Chicago White Sox who pitched for the Islanders in 1986, three years after his big league career was over. "Barry was a young guy trying to get to the big leagues. The difference was, you knew this guy was going to make it. He had the talent."

Tommy Sandt, who later became a coach with the Pirates, was the Islanders manager in 1986. He could tell immediately that Barry Bonds was no ordinary ballplayer. "It was like 'Wow, this is a big league player,'" Sandt said. "Put him in the lineup every day, that's all I had to do."

Yet sometimes that was risky. The Islanders were facing the Kansas City Royals' Class AAA team, and Bonds hit a line drive back at the pitcher that nearly took his head off. Bonds made fun of the pitcher's near miss, yelling at him as he ran to first base. Back in the Islanders' dugout, Sandt took Bonds aside.

"Barry, you've got a big name, you're a top draft choice and there's going to be a lot of jealous people out there and a lot of Triple-A players on their way out who would just love to take your head off," Sandt warned Bonds. "Don't give them a reason."

"They can't hit me anyhow," Bonds said.

The Islanders were playing in Phoenix in late May, and Pittsburgh general manager Syd Thrift was in the stands to watch some of the prospects. He had heard that other teams were pitching around Bonds rather than throw anything in the strike zone. He also had heard about Bonds' showboating: how the young outfielder flipped his bat after home runs and admired the ball as it sailed out of the park.

Before the game began, Thrift, a jocular man with a gentle Virginia drawl, watched the slender Bonds during batting practice. Bonds, a left-handed batter, promptly hit four or five balls over the right field fence, each traveling about a mile, then walked over to where Thrift was sitting.

"What do you think?" Bonds said.

"That's okay," Thrift said, "but let me see you hit them over the other fence."

So Bonds walked back to home plate and responded by hitting three or four balls over the left field fence. It was that easy for him.

The game started and Thrift could not take his eyes off the left fielder. Bonds was clearly a superior athlete and more self-assured than anyone else on the field, but he needed some polishing. He didn't have a strong arm, he sometimes misjudged a pitcher's timing while on the bases, and he wasn't going to jump in and bat .300 against big league pitchers. But at the time, Trench Davis was starting in left field for the Pirates and hitting about .130.

"If you were in Pittsburgh," Thrift said to Sandt, "who would you rather have, Barry Bonds or Trench Davis in the outfield?"

"Barry," Sandt said, without hesitating.

Thrift watched a few at-bats. In the sixth, inning he called Sandt over.

"Tommy, take him out of the game now," Thrift said. "He's going back with me to Pittsburgh. I've seen enough."

4

A MOST VALUABLE PLAYER

"He's only human."
— Bobby Bonds

After a half season at Class A and just 44 games at the Class AAA level, Barry Bonds was called up to the big leagues in late May 1986. Not everything went his way: he was assigned No. 7 and didn't like it. "My number is 24; it has been all my life," Bonds said. "I was born on the 24th of July and besides, my favorite player has always been Willie Mays," who wore 24. But utility player Denny Gonzalez had been assigned No. 24 in spring training and would not give up the number until the following season.

Pirates hitting coach Bill Virdon watched the 21-year-old Bonds swing with ease and power. "He's a natural swinger," Virdon said. "I don't want people to expect miracles but he has great potential."

Bonds had started slowly at Hawaii, striking out nearly once in every four at-bats, but he had reduced that to once every eight at-bats in the three weeks prior to being called up. Yet he never doubted his ability. "I had to take some time out, talk to my father, try some things," Bonds said. "Usually when I have trouble, it's because I'm doing some dumb little thing wrong."

Pirates manager Jim Leyland didn't hesitate, naming Bonds his starting center fielder on May 30.

Bonds launches a home run off Atlanta pitcher Tom Glavine in Game 6 of the 1992 NLCS to start an 8-run second inning.

In his second big league game, Bonds notched his first major league hit: a double off Rick Honeycutt of the Los Angeles Dodgers. On June 4, he belted his first home run off Atlanta's Craig McMurtry and, desperate to fit in with his big league teammates, bought pizzas for the team to celebrate. On September 24, he hit his 16th and final homer of the season, a ninth inning two-run shot for a come-from-behind win over Philadelphia.

"I've had game-winning hits before," Bonds said, "but never anything like this. This is what I dreamed of all my life."

He finished that year first among National League rookies in homers, RBI, stolen bases and walks, but also struck out 102 times in 113 games. Leyland could see that Bonds had all the physical attributes and skill to be an outstanding big league player. It was up to Bonds to make the necessary adjustments.

"He's going to get a lot of attention over the next two years," Leyland said. "How he handles that emotionally and mentally is going to be a big key to whether he becomes a superstar."

Bonds also had to learn to be a part of the team. From the start, he acted as if he'd played in the big leagues 16 years and batted .300 in 15 of them.

"He's his own biggest enemy," Pirates pitcher Rick Reuschel said. "Maybe it's because he has so much talent, but everything has come too easy for him. He doesn't have what it takes when it comes to listening and learning from other people. I can understand his wanting to try everything first, doing it his way, but it shouldn't be to the exclusion of getting help from other people."

Bonds opened the 1987 season in center field for the Pirates, but the team had acquired Andy Van Slyke at the end of spring training that year and Leyland started Van Slyke in center and switched Bonds to left on May 30. He batted .261 with 25 home runs.

Prior to his third major league season, Bonds settled down personally by marrying Sun, a woman he had met in Montreal the previous year. Bonds showed a little more improvement at the plate in 1988, batting .283. But in 1989, he slumped to .248. Even though Bonds acted like a know-it-all, he needed time to feel he belonged in the big leagues, that he was good enough to play there. "You just don't walk into the big leagues and tear it up right away, no matter how good you are," Leyland said. "No matter how highly touted you are, it takes time to get acclimated to the major leagues and the pressure of playing in the major leagues and I think Barry was a perfect example."

His fifth season in the big leagues, 1990, was his breakthrough year. He finally quieted his critics and put together a 30–30 season, just like his father, Bobby Bonds, did in the early 1970s for the Giants. Pittsburgh won the National League East in 1990, but neither the team nor Bonds did well in the playoffs. The Pirates faced the Cincinnati Reds in the National League Championship Series and lost the best-of-seven showdown, four games to two. Bonds hit just .167 with only one RBI. The Reds would go on to win the World Series, beating Oakland in four straight games.

"The reason why he struggled," former Pirates teammate Bobby Bonilla said, "is that he wanted to be the very best."

Bonds did receive his first Most Valuable Player award that year, and felt that what he had done over the season was more important than six postseason games. He wanted the Pirates to reward him. But for the second straight year, his salary was determined by an arbitrator who again ruled in favor of the team's $2.3 million offer. Bonds had wanted $3.25 million and publicly vowed not to re-sign with the Pirates after the season even "if they offered me $100 million."

Bonds' unhappiness boiled over on a characteristically sunny March day in Bradenton, Florida, where the Pirates held their spring training camp. The incident started over a trivial item: Bonds wanted a personal photographer allowed on the field and refused to be photographed by anyone else. Another photographer tried to take his picture and Bonds exploded, yelling at anyone within range. A television camera was present and caught the outburst on tape as well as Bonds' shouting match with Pirates manager Jim Leyland. A patient man who normally disciplined his players in private, Leyland was tired of Bonds' pouting. "I don't care what his problems are," Leyland said about his sulking superstar. "He's not going to run this camp. He can just go home."

But Bonds did not go home. Instead, he settled his differences with the manager and players, and apologized. "I will never let Jim Leyland down," Bonds said. "I say certain things out of frustration and anger because I feel I'm not getting my fair, just due. But Jim Leyland, that man has been too good to me. He's treated me with the greatest respect. We never had a major problem. Not before we had that shouting match, not after it."

In 1991, Bonds channeled his energy onto the field and the Pirates prospered. Pittsburgh

was in first place in the National League East in August despite losing 11 of its last 15 games. They had a six-game lead over St. Louis when the Cardinals came to town on August 12. After St. Louis took a 3–2 lead in the 11th inning. Lee Smith, St. Louis' behemoth closer at 6-foot 6-inches and 260 pounds, came in to face the heart of the Pirates: Van Slyke, Bonilla and Bonds. They were a combined 3-for-34 against Smith.

Van Slyke flew out, but Bonilla singled, and the crowd of 26,328 rose to its feet, chanting, "Bar-ree, Bar-ree." The first pitch to Bonds was a ball. The second was a called-strike fastball at the knees that Bonds never saw. The count went full to 3–2. "I'm hoping if he throws me another fastball that maybe I can hit it into left field," Bonds would say later. But Smith threw a slider in and Bonds connected, launching the ball out of the ballpark for a home run. The Pirates won 4–3 in extra innings. "The pitch wasn't even a strike," Smith said.

"Hitting a game-winning home run off Lee Smith is almost impossible," said Bonds, who had done the impossible. The Pirates surged, winning the division by 14 games. Bonds hit .292 that season with 25 home runs and 116 RBI, stealing 43 bases. But he finished second in the MVP voting to Terry Pendleton, who led the league with a .319 batting average and helped the Cinderella Atlanta Braves complete their rise from last place in 1990 to first place in the West in '91. The sportswriters casting the MVP ballots were supposed to base their decision on a player's performance, but Pendleton may have influenced a few votes because he was a genuinely nice guy. Terry Pendleton never yelled at anyone in public.

"I'll tip my hat and say congratulations," Bonds said. "Winning it [the MVP] makes you determined to do it again. Losing makes you even more determined to win."

The Pirates, repeat Eastern Division Champions, faced the pitching-rich Atlanta Braves in the NLCS. The Braves had prepared for Bonds.

"You don't want to let him beat you," Atlanta pitcher Tom Glavine said. "In an ideal world, you sit there as a pitcher and you say to yourself, 'All right, you have Barry Bonds in the lineup and I'm going to do my darndest to make sure he comes up every time with two outs and nobody on.' Or, you'd like him leading off the inning so if he hits a home run, it's a solo home run and hopefully that's not going to hurt you."

The postseason was a problem. Bonds again struggled, batting a dismal .148 and failing to drive in a single run. Pittsburgh lost, four games to three.

After the 1991 season, the Pirates took a deep breath. It was time for a third salary arbitration hearing with Bonds. This time, he asked for $5 million and the Pirates offered $4 million, the most ever offered by a team in an arbitration case. But before a hearing was held, the two sides reached an agreement; the Pirates would pay Bonds $4.7 million, then the highest one-year contract in baseball history.

Now it was time to put up or shut up. And Bonds produced. He hit .311, and posted his second 30-30 season, stealing 39 bases and hitting a career-high 34 home runs. Bonds ranked among the National League's best in batting average, home runs, RBI, doubles, walks and stolen bases.

Leyland knew what an intimidating player Bonds was—and he needed him in left field. "When I think about Barry, I think more of his defense than his offense," Leyland said. "I don't think any other left fielder could make the plays he made."

Feeling the pain of defeat, Bonds sits in his locker after the Atlanta Braves came from behind to win Game 7 of the 1992 NLCS, 3-2, in the ninth inning. His father never played in a World Series.

"If he isn't hitting," Bonilla said, "he'll make sure you don't get a hit. The way he plays defense separates Barry Bonds from everyone else."

There was the game against the Dodgers when Brett Butler sliced a ball over the third base bag and it rolled near the stands at Three Rivers Stadium in Pittsburgh. Somehow Bonds caught up with the ball and held the speedy Butler to a single. If anyone else had been in left, Butler would have had a double easily. "It was one of the most unbelievable plays I've ever seen," Leyland said.

If Bonds was struggling at the plate, and that did not happen often, he never let his frustration show in the outfield. Instead, he took hits away, climbing outfield walls to grab potential home runs and using his incredible speed to chase down balls. "I marvel that Barry Bonds was one of the few players I've ever seen who, when he's not hitting, is a better defensive player," Leyland said.

For the third straight year, the Pirates won the National League East. Atlanta was waiting. In the first two games of the NLCS, Bonds had one hit in six at-bats and the Pirates were trailing the Braves 2–0. Bonds was devastating in the regular season and disastrous in the postseason. "Barry Bonds is trying to hit a five-run homer every time he comes up," Leyland said. "He's trying to make unbelievable plays."

The Braves also made sure Bonds never got anything to hit and pitched around him in the series. His father, Bobby Bonds, could see what was happening. "Give my boy a chance," Bobby Bonds said. "He's only human."

The expectations were magnified because of Bonds' bravado and his big paycheck. His father, though, found some positive from the criticism.

"Maybe this is kind of good for him because it shows how much the people expect of him," Bobby Bonds said. "They respect his ability and his high standards."

Barry did rally, and hit .261 in the seven-game series. Pittsburgh had a 2–1 lead going into the ninth inning of the final game of the best-of-seven series, and was on the verge of its first World Series since 1979. But pinch-hitter Francisco Cabrera hit a two-run single to give Atlanta a 3–2 victory and the series.

"A lot of people would say Barry choked in the playoffs," Glavine said, "but I don't think that's the case. I think in the playoffs, Barry tried to do a little more than he has to, tried to be a better player than he already is."

Bonds was the best player in the game in 1992, winning his second MVP award in three years. "I think this is probably the most important one," Barry said, "because this one I'm giving to my mom. She deserves it."

He became the 10th player to win the National League award at least twice. But Bonds wasn't finished. "I want to do it again," Bonds said. "I'm 28. I want to be the first to do it four times."

He just wasn't going to do it in Pittsburgh.

5

SAN FRANCISCO

"He's the best player in the game."
— Darren Daulton

Bonds flips his bat in the air after striking out. Considered by many other players to be the best in the game, he can be warm and friendly, or rude and abusive, making him less popular than admired on and off the field.

The San Francisco Giants struggled in 1992, finishing 26 games behind Atlanta in the National League West with a 72–90 record. Some changes were necessary, and the Giants started with new ownership. The owners then selected a new manager, Dusty Baker, who had played with Atlanta, Los Angeles, San Francisco and Oakland. Baker played in three World Series with the Dodgers. He knew what it took to win.

The Giants needed some power. None of their outfielders had driven in more than 57 runs or hit more than 14 home runs in 1992. Barry Bonds was a free agent, which meant he could sign with any team he wanted. And Bonds wanted two things: money and a long-term contract, which would mean respect and security.

The Pittsburgh Pirates, a small-market team with limited financial resources, could not compete in the bidding for Bonds. His arrogance was not a factor. Pirates manager Jim Leyland felt Bonds was easy to manage.

"When you get a superstar—and Barry is certainly a superstar—who you can write in the lineup every day and never have to worry about, what else could a manager want?" Leyland said. "I don't care if we had a squabble every now and then. That doesn't bother me. I've managed a lot of good players and the one bonus in all of them is that they played every day. Barry Bonds came to the park every day and he played."

The Giants' new ownership, anxious to show Bay Area fans that they were serious about winning, needed a marquee name. They decided to invest in Bonds and offered a record six-year, $43.75 million contract. Bonds eagerly said yes, and not just because of the money. He would be back in San Francisco, playing in a ballpark he had grown up in, and wearing No. 24, the same uniform as his childhood hero and godfather, Willie Mays.

"It's like a boyhood dream that's come true for me," Bonds said about playing for the Giants. "This is the greatest moment in my entire life."

Baseball wasn't just a game to Bonds, it was a business. His new teammates were impressed. "What a difference he makes," said Giants reliever Rod Beck. "He can flat play. He doesn't get excited, either. We win, he sits down with his lunch, showers and goes home. It's business as usual. He expects it of himself, so why shouldn't we?"

Giants pitcher John Burkett noticed a difference in the clubhouse. "Just having Barry here—just the way he walks around. He's got an attitude. I think it's a great attitude."

What a difference his attitude made. He made a dazzling first impression by hitting a home run in his first at bat in the Giants' home opener on April 12, one of seven he hit that month to go along with his .431 average, resulting in National League Player of the Month honors. He hit two home runs in one game against New York, prompting Mets manager Jeff Torborg to say: "Bonds belongs in a higher league."

Pirates fans were not as kind. In his first game back wearing a Giants uniform on April 9, he was greeted by boos and buckets of fake dollar bills. Bonds went 2-for-4 with a double and triple and scored three runs. "All he's ever wanted—it's like his religion—is to be judged by what he's done on the field," former Pirates teammate Andy Van Slyke said of Bonds.

One player cannot carry a whole team, but Bonds' worth could be measured during the final six weeks of the season when the Giants lost eight straight games. Bonds struggled with his first and only slump of the season, and when he came out of it—hitting .333 in his final 16 games of the season—the Giants did, too, winning 14 of their last 17 games to finish with 103 victories. It just was not enough. San Francisco finished one game behind Atlanta in the West in the last year before expanded playoffs and restructured divisions.

Bonds was not happy about failing to win the West but he seemed to have found a new home. "My teammates really took to me differently," Bonds said. "It wasn't about how you dressed or what you said—it was about how you play the game. They saw this guy play hard and work out every day. They said, 'This kid doesn't play for the money. He plays to be better than everybody.'"

In his first season in San Francisco, Bonds was better than everybody. He hit a career-high .336 and led the National League in homers (46) and RBI (123). He became the first player since Stan Musial in 1948 to lead the league in both on-base percentage and slugging percentage. He won his fourth Gold Glove award, presented to the top defensive players in the game, and for the third time in four years, Bonds was named Most Valuable Player.

"There's no question who the MVP is," said Giants shortstop Royce Clayton.

His name was now linked to seven Hall of Fame players. Bonds was the first player ever to win the MVP award three times in four seasons, and joined Jimmie Foxx, Joe DiMaggio, Stan Musial, Roy Campanella, Yogi Berra, Mickey Mantle and Mike Schmidt as one of only eight players to win three MVPs.

"I can't say I'm ranked with the Hall of Famers yet," Bonds said. "I know how good those guys were."

Despite the less than welcome greeting by Pittsburgh fans upon his return, Bonds remained a legend there. "He did everything so easy," said Al Martin, who replaced Bonds in left field in 1993 for the Pirates. "I don't think people realize how good he really is. When the ball's hit to him and he does his catches—he calls his 'snatch'—you always know he's on the field. I'm just a grunt type of player. I go out and do the best job I know how. He was fun to watch and it's fun for me to be able to say I was the guy who played left field after him because he's going to go down in history as one of the best left fielders in the game."

Martin cannot play a single game without being reminded of Bonds. "Barry himself always said, 'You'll never be the best one to wear that uniform in left,'" Martin said.

Some players might consider that taunting, but Martin looked at Bonds' brashness differently. "He's trying to help me out, motivate me," Martin said. "I'll always hear people say 'You're not Bonds' or 'Why are you wearing high tops?' or something like that. It doesn't bother me. I just go out and play hard. He's a legend."

Barry Bonds sometimes treated people as if they were an opposing fastball. Off the field, he was mercurial. Bonds could be friendly and charming, or rude and abusive. The fans were dazzled by his skill, and justifiably so. Should his personality interfere with how people think of him as a ballplayer? It was a question Barry and his father had dealt with throughout their baseball careers.

A fourth Most Valuable Player award was on Bonds' wish list for the 1994 season. He battled through a bone spur in his right elbow in early May and appeared to be on the verge of better

Michael Jordan, shown here at the 1993 All-Star celebrity home run contest, listens as Barry Bonds explains why being a basketball superstar does not mean you can hit a curve. Jordan abandoned his attempt to become a major league ballplayer after a short stint in the minor leagues in 1994.

power numbers than in 1993. But the players went on strike August 12, wiping out the final seven weeks of the season.

Baseball's labor problems took center stage rather than the incredible offensive outbursts that were being played in major league ballparks. Ken Griffey Jr. and Matt Williams were chasing Roger Maris' single-season record of 61 home runs set in 1961; Joe Carter was in pursuit of Hack Wilson's RBI record of 190 set in 1930; Frank Thomas was closing in on Babe Ruth's record for most runs in a season of 177 set in 1921. But the strike silenced all the talk. In all, 668 regular season games were lost, along with the canceled postseason games and the World Series, which had been played every year since 1905. "I honestly believe baseball is never going to be the same," said Los Angeles outfielder Brett Butler after the World Series was called off.

Bonds hit 37 home runs in the shortened season, a pace that would have produced 52 in a full season. The National League record was 56 set by Hack Wilson in 1930. Williams, Bonds' teammate, was leading the majors with 43 homers when the strike was called on August 12. Postseason awards were still presented, and Houston's Jeff Bagwell, who led the league in RBI and runs scored, unanimously won MVP while Bonds finished fourth.

Baseball resumed play in 1995 because of a judge's order in March requiring the two sides to continue under the old labor agreement. Bonds focused on the game. He had started the two previous seasons batting fifth, but Giants manager Dusty Baker moved him to third in the lineup ahead of Williams. However, when Williams was sidelined for 68 games with a foot injury, pitchers could work around Bonds in the lineup. When Williams was present, Bonds hit .305 and walked 53 times. Without Williams, Bonds hit .282 and drew 67 walks.

That year marked the first time Bonds did not hit .300—he finished with a .294 average—since 1991. But he did achieve a personal milestone. On September 21 at Coors Field against Colorado Rockies pitcher Jeff Grahe, Bonds hit his 30th home run of the season. The next day in Colorado, he stole his 30th base to become the Giants' first 30-30 player since his father Bobby Bonds had done so in 1973. Barry finished with 33 home runs and 31 stolen bases, his third 30–30 season.

Barry and Bobby Bonds represented the ultimate show of power and speed in a father-son pair. Following the 1995 season, the two held the major league record for home runs and stolen bases by a father-son combination with 624 homers and 801 stolen bases combined.

"He's the best player in the game," Philadelphia catcher Darren Daulton said. "And it's not even close."

6

THE REGGIE JACKSON OF THE '90S

"I don't want to be king of the world."
— Barry Bonds

Barry Bonds was a force for the San Francisco Giants. He was most dangerous with runners on base. From 1991 through 1995, Bonds hit .329 with runners in scoring position. Opposing managers worried about Bonds even before he stepped up to the plate. "The situation you hate is when there's a man on first and second, and you can't intentionally walk him," Chicago Cubs manager Jim Riggleman said. "If a guy like that makes the last out in the seventh, then you think you've got a chance to not see him again that game."

During a Cubs-Giants game May 17, 1995 at San Francisco, young right-handed pitcher Kevin Foster had a 1–0 lead going into the seventh inning against the Giants. There were two outs and Robby Thompson was batting. Bonds was on deck. If Foster got Thompson out, Bonds would lead off the next inning with nobody on base. Instead, Foster walked Thompson and Bonds stepped up and homered. The Giants won 2–1.

Riggleman had considered another option. He was thinking about making a double switch and moving Foster, the pitcher, to third base. He could then call on left-handed reliever Larry Casian to

Bonds waits his turn at bat in full modern dress, complete with batting gloves and personalized wrist bands. The metal rings on the bat make it heavier during practice swings; the bat then feels lighter than its actual weight when they are removed.

49

face the left-handed batting Bonds—and not take Foster out of the game. That may seem extreme, but the chances of Bonds hitting the ball to third were slim to none and Foster was an infielder before being converted to a pitcher. Once Casian got Bonds out, Riggleman could then switch Foster back to his regular spot.

But Riggleman did not do that. "It looks like you're trying to be cute," he said, "but Barry Bonds is the type of guy who would make you do that."

And it was not just Bonds' hitting that worried managers. If he was on second base, it was almost automatic that he would score on a single hit anywhere in the park. "He's a very good base runner," Riggleman said. "When he's leading off and you put him on, he steals and beats you that way." In the outfield, Bonds could get to a ball quicker than most other players and make up for a less than spectacular arm with his footspeed.

At every team meeting before facing Bonds, pitcher Mike Morgan said there was one message: Don't let him beat you.

"He's a tough out," said Morgan, who pitched for the Dodgers, Cubs, Cardinals and Reds. "He still makes seven outs every 10 at-bats. You just hope you're the guy who gets him four of those seven times."

Bonds' arrogance never bothered Morgan. Most players respect great talent.

"He's the Reggie Jackson of the '90s," Morgan said of Bonds. "He's a great player and I'll always say that no matter what he says or does."

Heading into the 1996 season, Bonds was eight home runs shy of 300 in his career. His personal life had changed: the father of two children, 6-year-old son Nikolai and 4-year-old

daughter Shikari, Barry divorced his wife Sun
prior to spring training. He had spent the off-
season in the weight room, this time under the
guidance of personal trainer Raymond Fariss,
who also supervised NFL players Jerry Rice and
Roger Craig. Bonds arrived in the Giants camp
leaner—his body fat dropped from 12 percent to 8
percent—and more muscular—he could bench
press 315 pounds, up from 230. And Fariss made
Bonds constantly run sprints to improve his speed.

But doing a zillion bicep curls will not
guarantee success on the field. Bonds had great
baseball instincts, which cannot be developed
in a weight room. "He sees things quicker than
any other player except Hank Aaron," Giants
manager Dusty Baker said. "He sees a pitcher
flaring his glove on a changeup and he'll come

*Dusty Baker, a 19-year
veteran who played in
three World Series with
the Los Angeles Dodgers,
became the Giants' man-
ager in 1993, the year
Barry Bonds joined them.
Baker knew what it took
to win, and Bonds had an
immediate impact on the
team, but they were
unable to win a pennant
in their first four years
together.*

back to the dugout and say, 'Did you see that?' Other guys don't see that until the sixth inning, if they see it at all."

Bonds is modest about his skills. "I just know the game well, I guess," he said. "I don't try to evaluate every little thing that other people are doing. I just try to keep myself mechanically sound and if they make a mistake and put the ball within that little square [of his strike zone], then if I'm mechanically sound, it doesn't really make a difference what they throw."

Bonds showed off his fundamentally correct swing during the home run hitting contest on a sweltering July day before the 1996 All-Star Game in Philadelphia. Some of the most powerful hitters in baseball took part, including Seattle's Jay Buhner and Baltimore's Brady Anderson. But the finals came down to a Battle of the Bay between San Francisco area players: Bonds and Oakland's Mark McGwire. McGwire grounded out twice before hitting his first home run to left, then hit another. Both were towering drives.

Bonds was next. He took the first pitch from Phillies coach Dave Cash, then hit the next pitch into the upper deck in right and followed that with another homer almost in the same spot. Bonds then smashed a third home run to right and McGwire literally threw in the towel, tossing one from the dugout and surrendering to Bonds. "I did it—I beat the great Mark McGwire," said Bonds, sounding like a little kid gloating after a game of king of the hill.

But Bonds was not a home run hitter. "I think of Barry as a line drive hitter with power," Baker said. "Most of the good hitters are like that. I could never see him being a true bona fide slugger who's going to strike out 130 times and hit 35 home runs. He wouldn't be satisfied with that."

Yet in 1996, Bonds joined Jose Canseco as the only players in baseball to hit 40 home runs and steal 40 bases in the same season. "I wouldn't recommend anyone trying this," Bonds joked. "My legs are getting sore from running every day." Bonds had to hurry to reach the milestone. He hit his 40th home run on September 16, finishing with 42, and stole 15 bases for the month.

Barry Bonds poses with his children, Shikari, 2, on the left, and Nikolai, 3, on Father's Day 1993. "I spend as much time with my kids as I can, especially in the morning before I go to the ballpark," said Bonds, whose marriage ended in a divorce in 1996.

In 1996 Barry Bonds joined (from left) Willie Mays; Bobby Bonds; and Andre Dawson as the only players to hit at least 300 home runs and steal 300 bases. Bobby and Barry Bonds also hold the father & son home run record.

"Barry never had a finer season," Giants general manager Bob Quinn said.

Bonds hit .308, scored 122 runs and drove in 129. Despite playing in a patchwork lineup, he still led the majors with 151 walks. The Giants had to scrap all season because of injuries to key players. They fielded their opening day lineup only three times all year, all in the first week of play, and finished 23 games behind the San Diego Padres in the West. Failing to reach the playoffs was not the only disappointment that year for Bonds. His father, who had been a Giants coach since 1993, was fired in October. Barry was said to be angry at the move, especially because he had to learn about it secondhand. His agents said he wanted to be traded. One source told the San Francisco *Chronicle*, "He's upset that they didn't call him or discuss it with him. They fired his father. If somebody fired your

father, how would you feel?" The Giants offered Bobby Bonds another position.

After losing 94 games, the Giants needed overhauling. They were looking forward to playing in a new ballpark to be built in downtown San Francisco. But the first priority was to put a better team on the field. Six teams expressed an interest in Barry Bonds, including the Florida Marlins, where his old manager at Pittsburgh, Jim Leyland, was now the skipper. But the Giants kept Bonds, and traded third baseman, Matt Williams, who had batted behind Bonds in the lineup. This left Bonds, who had finished fifth in the MVP voting, with little protection in the batting order. The Giants sought to fill that hole by aquiring two-time Gold Glove first baseman J. T. Snow from California.

If the Giants had any hopes of reaching postseason play, they would need another monumental year from Bonds. The 1996 season was his tenth in the majors; he had yet to make it to the World Series. Some stars—Ernie Banks, Luke Appling, Ralph Kiner and Don Mattingly, to name a few— had played for many years without making it to a World Series. Bonds did not want to join that group. No matter what anybody said about him— arrogant, distant—he was a team player who wanted to win.

"You hear them say that Barry Bonds is one of the best players in the game today," he said, "but I'll never be in the elite category until I win [a World Series]. I have the God-given ability to be a contender, to be a big piece of the puzzle, but so far that's all I have."

Winning a championship had eluded him since high school. His Serra High team reached the sectional championships three times and lost. His Arizona State team played in two College World Series and lost. The Pirates won the East three times, but lost the NLCS each year.

"I don't want to be king of the world," Bonds said. "I'm not doing this for the money; I think you can tell that by the way I play. And I'm not comfortable being at the center of things, getting all the attention. I don't need that. I appreciate all the ability I've been given but all I want to do is win."

But if Bonds was to win a world championship, it would depend not just on him, but on his team. As a player, he had won the respect of baseball people. "The best player I ever saw when I was playing was Willie Mays," said veteran coach and manager, Don Zimmer. "But Bonds can be rated with the best of them—Mays, [Roberto] Clemente. A lot of people won't give him the credit that's due him because of the way he acts, but Barry Bonds is a tremendous player. Nobody can play left field any better, steal a base, hit home runs."

To win another MVP award, Bonds would have to put together an incredible season. "If you're more consistent than anybody in the National League and you do the same thing for five years, sometime around the third year there's no glamour to it," said San Diego's Tony Gwynn. "In Barry Bonds' case, it might take a 50–50 for him to be an MVP again. That, and the fact that he could do that and his team would probably have to win, too."

But trying to hit 50 home runs in one season might result in a drop in his batting average, which does not interest Bonds. "I like 30–30 and hitting .300 and driving in 100 runs and scoring 100." he said. "To me, that's as complete as you can get."

Barry Bonds had achieved one goal in life: he had moved out of his father's shadow. He was no longer Bobby Bonds' son, burdened with great expectations. He had become baseball's most complete player, and had established his own standards for his—or other players'—sons to strive for.

CHRONOLOGY

1964 Born Barry Lamar Bonds in Riverside, California, on July 24

1982 Selected by San Francisco in second round of June draft but decides to attend Arizona State University on a baseball scholarship

1985 Drafted by the Pittsburgh Pirates in the first round and joins Class A Prince William of the Carolina League

1986 Plays only 44 games at Class AAA level in Hawaii before being called up to majors; hits first major league home run on June 4

1990 Wins National League Most Valuable Player award after becoming second player in major league history to hit 30 home runs and steal 50 bases in the same season

1992 Wins second MVP award after hitting .311 with 34 home runs and 39 stolen bases; becomes a free agent after the season and signs record six-year, $43.75 million contract with San Francisco Giants

1993 Captures third MVP award in spectacular first season with Giants, batting .336 with 46 home runs and driving in 123 runs; collects 1,000th hit on April 18 and 200th home run on July 8

1994 Wins fifth consecutive Gold Glove award

1995 Becomes Giants' first 30-30 player since his father Bobby Bonds did so in 1973, hitting 33 home runs and stealing 31 bases

1996 Hits 300th and 301st home runs on April 27 off Florida's John Burkett; becomes second player in major league history to record 40–40 season

MAJOR LEAGUE STATISTICS

PITTSBURGH PIRATES, SAN FRANCISCO GIANTS

YEAR	TEAM	G	AB	R	H	2B	3B	HR	RBI	BA	SB
1986	Pit N	113	413	72	92	26	3	16	48	.223	36
1987		150	551	99	144	34	9	25	59	.261	32
1988		144	538	97	152	30	5	24	58	.283	17
1989		159	580	96	144	34	6	19	58	.248	32
1990		151	519	104	156	32	3	33	114	.301	52
1991		153	510	95	149	28	5	25	116	.292	43
1992		140	473	109	147	36	5	34	103	.311	39
1993	SF N	159	539	129	181	38	4	46	123	.336	29
1994		112	391	89	122	18	1	37	81	.312	29
1995		144	506	109	149	30	7	33	104	.294	31
1996		158	517	122	159	27	3	42	129	.308	40
Totals		1583	5537	1121	1595	333	51	334	993	.288	380

FURTHER READING

Ekin, Larry. *Baseball Fathers, Baseball Sons.* Cincinnati: Betterway Books, 1992.

Harvey, Miles. *Barry Bonds: Baseball's Complete Player.* Chicago: Children's Press, 1994.

Goodman, Michael. *Pittsburgh Pirates.* Mankato, MN: Creative Education, 1992.

Gowdy, David. *Baseball's Super Stars.* New York: Putnam, 1994.

Kramer, Sydelle A. *Baseball's Greatest Hitters.* New York: Random Books for Young Readers, 1995.

INDEX

PICTURE CREDITS
AP/Wide World Photos: pp. 14, 30, 35, 37, 40, 45, 53, 54; Arizona State University: p. 22; National Baseball Library and Archive, Cooperstown NY: pp. 8, 26, 51, 58; Photo File: p. 2; Pittsburgh Pirates: p. 11; Mike Rucki: p. 48; Transcendental Graphics: p. 17.

CARRIE MUSKAT has covered major league baseball since 1981, beginning with United Press International in Minneapolis. She was UPI's lead writer at the 1991 World Series. A freelance journalist since 1992, she is a regular contributor to *USA Today* and *USA Today Baseball Weekly*. Her work also has appeared in the *Chicago Tribune, Inside Sports* and *ESPN Total Sports* magazine.

JIM MURRAY, veteran sports columnist of the *Los Angeles Times,* is one of America's most acclaimed writers. He has been named "America's Best Sportswriter" by the National Association of Sportscasters and Sportswriters 14 times, was awarded the Red Smith Award, and was twice winner of the National Headliner Award. In addition, he was awarded the J. G. Taylor Spink Award in 1987 for "meritorious contributions to baseball writing." With this award came his 1988 induction into the National Baseball Hall of Fame in Cooperstown, New York. In 1990, Jim Murray was awarded the Pulitzer Prize for Commentary.

EARL WEAVER is the winningest manager in the Baltimore Orioles' history by a wide margin. He compiled 1,480 victories in his 17 years at the helm. After managing eight different minor league teams, he was given the chance to lead the Orioles in 1968. Under his leadership the Orioles finished lower than second place in the American League East only four times in 17 years. One of only 12 managers in big league history to have managed in four or more World Series, Earl was named Manager of the Year in 1979. The popular Weaver had his number, 5, retired in 1982, joining Brooks Robinson, Frank Robinson, and Jim Palmer, whose numbers were retired previously. Earl Weaver continues his association with the professional baseball scene by writing, broadcasting, and coaching.